Princess Adventures

Disney PRESS

Los Angeles • New York

Contents

The Secret of the Star Shell

ONE BRIGHT and sunny morning in the village, Ariel was giving her young friend Laurel a singing lesson.

"Why don't we try this one next?" Ariel said, pointing to a song in her music book.

Laurel's eyes sparkled. "'The Song of the Sea.' That reminds me of my new best friend!"

"What's your friend's name?" Ariel asked.

Laurel suddenly hesitated. "Um, I'm not sure you'd know her. I'm meeting her after our lesson. Maybe I'll sing her 'The Song of the Sea.'"

Later that afternoon, Ariel visited her sisters by the ocean. Ariel's sister Adella had brought her a present. It was a shimmering star-shaped shell with a delicate ribbon on top.

"It's beautiful!" Ariel gasped. "Where did you find it?"

"It was caught in the current," Adella said. "It's a star shell. It's supposed to grant wishes."

The sisters each took turns making a wish, but nothing happened.

"That's all right," Ariel said. She tied the ribbon around her neck to wear the shell as a necklace. "It's a beautiful gift. Now I'll carry a part of the sea wherever I go."

As Ariel walked back to the village, she passed Laurel's cottage. Suddenly, Laurel's father, Mr. Hansen, came running out.

"Princess Ariel! Is Laurel with you?" he asked. He sounded upset.

"No," Ariel said. "Has something happened?"

"Laurel went to play with a friend after your music lesson, but she never came back," Mr. Hansen explained. "I hope she hasn't gotten lost."

"Laurel mentioned that she'd made a new friend," Ariel said. "Maybe they're still playing and lost track of time. Perhaps there's a clue in her room about who this friend is and where we could find her!"

Together, Ariel and Mr. Hansen checked Laurel's room. On her desk, a pink journal lay open to an entry:

Dear Diary,

I met a new friend by the ocean. Her name is Calista! We've played together every day this week. She even gave me a beautiful necklace. Calista said not to tell anyone about our secret friendship. But that's okay—it's fun to have a secret friend. I'm going to buy her a treat from the bakery!

Ariel and Mr. Hansen split up to look for Laurel. Ariel hurried over to the pastry shop.

"Hmmm," the baker said when Ariel explained what had happened. "Yes, I do remember Laurel stopping by. She wanted seaweed puffs!"

Just then, a little girl named Maggie handed the baker a colorful card.

He smiled. "Why, it's a thank-you note!"

"It's part of a school assignment," Maggie's mother explained.

Ariel looked thoughtful. Maggie was in Laurel's class, which meant she would have had to write a thank-you note, too. Maybe she wrote one to Calista for the necklace!

At the school, the teacher showed Ariel the thank-you notes. Laurel's was written on a bright green card.

Dear Princess Ariel,

Thank you for helping me practice. It has been a big help. I hope you enjoy our concert. Your friend, Laurel

Ariel sighed. The card was lovely, but it wasn't a clue.

"Laurel loves to draw," the teacher said. "Yesterday I asked my students to make a picture of their best friend. Laurel couldn't wait to get started."

"Best friend!" Ariel exclaimed. Maybe she drew a picture of Calista!

The teacher handed Ariel the drawing labeled MY BEST FRIEND.

There were two girls in the drawing. One was Laurel; the other girl had wavy blond hair. It had to be Calista. And she was a mermaid!

Ariel thanked the teacher and ran back to Mr. Hansen's house. She quickly told him what she had discovered.

"Could Calista really be a mermaid?" Mr. Hansen asked.

"It makes sense," Ariel said. "Look at the clues. Laurel met her by the ocean. She bought her seaweed puffs. And Calista wanted to keep their friendship a secret. She must be a mermaid!"

"But then, where's my daughter?" Mr. Hansen said.

Ariel smiled. "I know just how to find out."

At the beach, Ariel called for her friends Flounder and Sebastian. They fetched Ariel's father, King Triton, to transform Ariel back into a mermaid.

In no time, Ariel was searching for Calista under the sea. Soon she and King Triton found Calista's family grotto. The young mermaid was there, and she was very nervous.

"You're not in trouble," Ariel said. "We just want to know where Laurel is. Her father is very worried."

"I don't want anyone to worry," Calista said. She led Ariel and Triton to her bedroom. Slowly, Laurel swam out from under Calista's bed.

Ariel gasped. "Laurel! You're here! And . . . you're a mermaid, too?"

Ariel was confused. What could have happened to transform Laurel? And how could they change her back?

"It's hard to explain." Laurel sniffled. "When I went to see Calista this morning, I was wearing my star shell necklace. As we were playing, I told Calista that I wished I could be a mermaid so we could play under the sea. All of a sudden, my necklace lit up and my legs became a tail!"

Calista nodded. "We realized the shell must be magical. So we thought we could just wish Laurel to be human again later."

"But when we were playing on the octopus slide," Laurel said, "my necklace got swept away in the current."

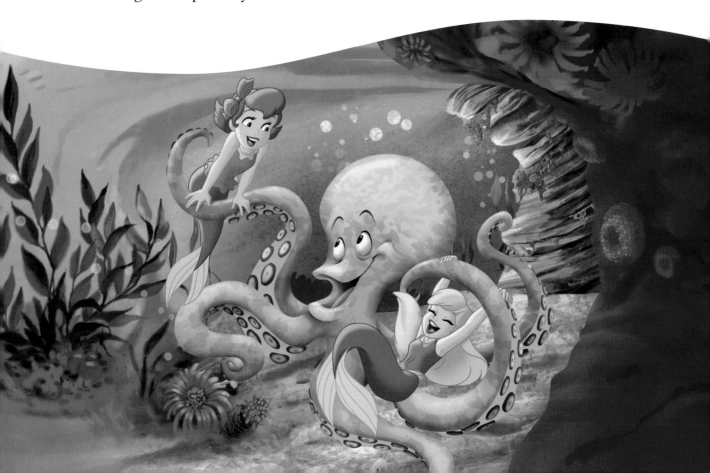

Suddenly, Calista spotted Ariel's star shell necklace. "You found it!" she said. "That means we can wish Laurel human again!"

Ariel looked at her father. King Triton smiled kindly.

"I'm afraid the Legend of the Star Shell works a little differently," he said. "Come with me to the surface, and I'll explain."

Above the water, King Triton held up the star shell.

"Star shells can only grant one wish," he said. "To undo this wish, the shell must be broken."

Calista turned to Laurel. "When you're human again, will you still visit me by the ocean?"

"Of course!" Laurel smiled.

Together, everyone swam back to shore. Ariel handed Laurel the star shell.

Laurel lifted the shell high up in the air, paused, and then brought it down against a large rock. With a burst of light, her mermaid tail changed back into legs.

Immediately, Mr. Hansen rushed over and hugged his daughter tight.

A few days later, Ariel asked Calista and Laurel to meet her by the water.

"I have presents for you both," Ariel said. She handed the girls two brand-new necklaces made from star shell pieces.

"They're beautiful," Laurel breathed.

"Thank you, Princess Ariel," Calista said.

Ariel smiled. "When I was wearing the star shell, it was like carrying part of the ocean with me. Now you two can always carry a piece of your adventure with you wherever you go."

Disney
PRINCESS
Cinderella
A New Mouse

WARM SUNLIGHT streamed through the windows of Cinderella's parlor as she and her mouse friends shared afternoon tea.

Even though the food was delicious, Cinderella found it difficult to enjoy the tasty treats. She was too busy thinking about her friend Gabrielle, who would be visiting very soon.

Just then, a royal page entered the parlor. "Lady Gabrielle has arrived," he announced.

Gabrielle swept into the room and ran to hug Cinderella.

"It's so good to see you, dear," she said.

As the two friends chatted excitedly, Jaq and Gus noticed that Gabrielle had an unusual item with her.

"What's-a that?" Jaq said. He pointed eagerly to a fancy little house.

Gabrielle noticed the curious mice and explained right away. "Let me introduce you to my beloved friend Babette." Gabrielle opened the little door to the house, and Babette walked onto her hand.

Jaq and Gus couldn't believe it. Babette was a mouse! They waved at Babette, but she just stared at them.

"Would you like a crumpet, Babette?" Cinderella asked.

The mouse took a piece and ran back onto Gabrielle's hand.

"She should-a said thank-a you," Jaq whispered to Gus.

"Rude!" Gus agreed.

"Cinderella, dear, you simply must show me the castle garden," Gabrielle said, setting down Babette.

"Jaq, Gus, perhaps you can give Babette a tour of the castle," Cinderella suggested.

Jaq and Gus agreed and immediately began showing Babette all their favorite places in the castle.

"This-a the library!" Jaq said.

"Lots-a books," Gus said, pointing up at the shelves.

Babette looked around but didn't say a word.

Then Jaq and Gus took Babette to the grand ballroom. "You have a ballroom?" Jaq asked, trying to start a conversation.

Babette nodded. And that was all.

Jaq and Gus took Babette all over the castle, hoping to find something she would be interested in. But no matter where they went, Babette just nodded or stayed silent.

Later Cinderella asked Jaq and Gus how their day with Babette had been.

"She's a snob," Jaq told Cinderella.

"Stuck up!" Gus agreed.

"Now, now," Cinderella said gently. "You hardly know her. Give her a chance."

As Cinderella set the pair of mice down on the ground, she noticed something was missing. "My bracelet!" she gasped. "It must have fallen off during Gabrielle's tour!"

"We can find it, Cinderelly!" Jaq said.

"Oh, thank you for offering," Cinderella said, "but we went all over the castle. The bracelet could be anywhere."

"No problem for Jaq and Gus-Gus!" Jaq said proudly. "Follow us, Cinderelly!"

Cinderella and the mice went to ask Gabrielle about the last time she remembered seeing the bracelet, but she couldn't remember.

"I can help you look," a soft voice said. It was Babette, stepping out of her little house.

Jaq and Gus looked suspiciously at Babette, but Cinderella spoke up for her. "That would be wonderful. Thank you, Babette!"

Gus and Jaq reluctantly agreed. "We check the mouse-size places and Cinderelly check the princess-size places."

The three mice scurried from room to room. They looked behind curtains, on top of cabinets, and even in the tea room. Gus checked inside an entire tea set.

"Gus-Gus, Cinderelly's bracelet isn't in a teapot," Jaq laughed.

Gus looked embarrassed, but Babette spoke up quietly. "It never hurts to check."

The mice continued searching the tea room until Babette let out a squeal of joy.

"Jaq! Gus! Look!" she cried. Babette had found Cinderella's bracelet stuck between two chair cushions.

"Hooray!" Gus and Jaq cheered.

The pair of mice hopped down to help Babette free the heavy bracelet from between the cushions.

"You can tell Cinderelly you found it!" Gus said.

"Oh, I couldn't," Babette said, blushing.

Suddenly, Gus and Jaq understood why Babette had been so quiet. She wasn't a snob. She was just shy!

"Cinderelly is the nicest princess ever," Jaq said. "You can talk to her."

The mice found Cinderella looking through her bedroom.

Jaq and Gus gently pushed Babette forward with the bracelet.

"Oh, you little dear!" Cinderella cried. "Did you find my bracelet?" Babette blushed and nodded.

"Thank you," Cinderella said.

Babette saw that she was surrounded by kind friends. She gathered all her courage, looked Cinderella in the eye, and said, "You're welcome, Princess."

Now that the bracelet had been found, the three mice decided to play together. They spent the rest of the day playing in the many castle rooms they had explored earlier.

But their fun couldn't last forever. When it was time for Gabrielle to go home, Jaq and Gus were very sorry to say good-bye to their new friend.

"Come back soon!" Gus said.

Babette waved. "I'll miss you!" she said.

When Gabrielle and Babette were out of sight, Jaq turned to Cinderella.
"Babette!" he said. "She's so much fun!"

"The best!" Gus chimed in.

"Oh, really?" Cinderella asked with a smile. "She's not 'stuck up' or a 'snob'?"

"We're sorry, Cinderelly," Jaq said.

"That's all right," Cinderella replied. "I'm sure you'll be more patient with new friends in the future."

"We sure will!" Jaq said as Gus nodded in agreement.

Disney PRINCESS

Tangled

The Sweetest Day Ever

RAPUNZEL WAS having the best birthday of her life. She'd finally left her tower. She and her chameleon, Pascal, had made some new friends—like Flynn, the well-meaning thief, and Maximus, the noble horse. In a few short hours, she'd get to see the floating lanterns she'd always wondered about.

And now they had time to explore the whole kingdom of Corona. Since that day was the celebration of the lost princess's birthday, the whole town was out and about for the festivities.

Rapunzel had never met so many interesting people. There were musicians playing lively tunes, kids drawing with chalk, and all sorts of street vendors selling goodies. Rapunzel found she had plenty to talk about with all of them.

"Hello, there!" a man called from behind a fruit stand. "Crispy, delicious apples? They're straight from my farm."

Rapunzel bounded up to greet him. "They certainly look delicious," she responded. "What's it like owning a farm?"

Farther down the street, Rapunzel got into a conversation with another vendor. "Wow! Are these your paintings? What types of brushes do you use?"

"I know a fellow artist when I see one," the painter said. The two started chatting like old friends.

Suddenly, Flynn and Rapunzel heard a commotion behind them.

"I have half a mind to call the palace guards!" a voice cried.

"Hey! A bakery!" Rapunzel said, heading for the door.

"Um . . . what was that about 'palace guards'?" Flynn asked nervously.
"Besides, I don't even like sweets!"

Despite Flynn's protests, Rapunzel followed her curiosity inside. Her attention was immediately drawn to the lively feud in front of her.

"I'm sorry, but we're all out!" a small man said.

"How can you be out, today of all days?" a flushed baker asked him. "How am I going to make my famous Lost Princess Cupcakes without milk and eggs?"

Rapunzel stepped forward. "Wait, you don't have eggs or milk?"

"That's right," the baker said, her eyes narrowing at Rapunzel.

"I can help! Stay right there," Rapunzel declared. And with that, she ran out of the bakery as fast as she could.

The baker and the dairyman turned to stare at the man left standing awkwardly nearby.

"Um . . . I guess I'll go help," Flynn said, darting out behind her.

First Rapunzel rushed back to the farmer's stand. Flynn, Maximus, and Pascal hurried behind her.

"Hi again, Frank! I need some of your finest!" Rapunzel grabbed as many apples as she could carry.

Then they stopped by the artist's corner. "You don't have any unused paintbrushes you could spare, do you, Felix?" Rapunzel asked.

Soon the girl, boy, horse, and chameleon were back at the bakery, their goods in tow.

The baker led Rapunzel into the kitchen, curious about what she was going to do.

"You don't need milk or eggs," Rapunzel announced. "You can use applesauce!"

"Applesauce?" the baker repeated.

"Yep!" Rapunzel taught the baker her favorite way of whipping up applesauce.

In no time, golden cupcakes were cooling on the counter. Then Rapunzel grabbed a borrowed paintbrush and decorated the cupcakes with colorful frosting.

"You saved the day!" the baker said. "Cupcakes for everyone. . .even you, Lester," she said, eyeing the dairyman. She handed Flynn a basket filled with the beautiful sweet treats.

Rapunzel and Flynn knew just where to take them. Saving the Lost Princess Cupcakes had been a team effort, after all.

Frank loved the sweet taste.

Felix loved the frosting decorations.

"I think I'll try one now, too," Rapunzel said, taking a cupcake out of the basket.

Suddenly, Flynn jumped, his eyes wide. "Run!" he shouted.

Rapunzel turned to see some guards heading in their direction. She squealed, and they sprinted away through the crowd.

Finally, they found a hidden corner, holding their breath as the guards ran past. When the coast was clear, they burst out laughing.

"I sure have worked up an appetite," Flynn said, grabbing a cupcake from the basket.

"I thought you didn't like sweets," Rapunzel teased.

"I'll make an exception this time," he said. "Wow! This is delicious."

"Thanks," Rapunzel said, taking a bite out of hers. They looked at each other for a moment, blushing and grinning.

As the sun started to set, Rapunzel thought about how truly sweet the day had been. . .and it wasn't over yet! Soon it would be time to see the floating lanterns, with her new friends at her side!

Disney PRINCESS

Beauty and the Beast

The Perfect Pearl

IT WAS a lazy afternoon at the Beast's castle, and Belle and Chip were exploring the library.

"What do you suppose is in this chest?" Belle asked the enchanted teacup.

"Books!" Chip replied.

Belle laughed. "I mean what kind of books, silly."

Belle threw open the doors. "I knew it. More beautiful adventures—tucked away and forgotten, maybe even unread!" she said.

It wasn't that the Beast didn't use the library. But when he did, he always read the same book.

"My library is your library," he liked to remind Belle. "Read and enjoy any book you find."

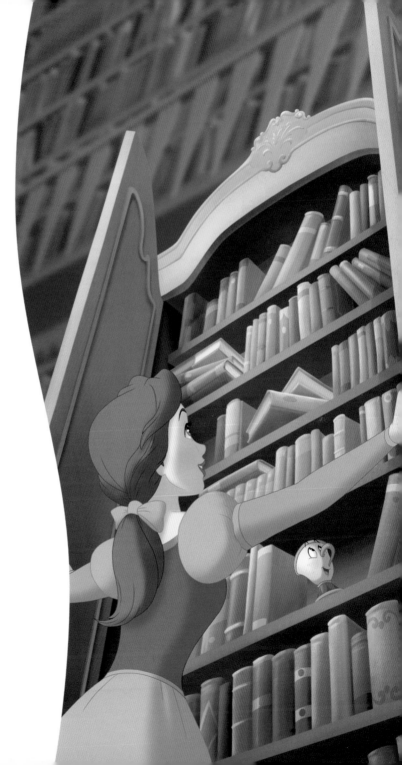

It hadn't been long since Belle had agreed to stay at the castle in return for her father's freedom. But each day she was getting to know the Beast better. She was starting to think that he actually cared about her happiness. So Belle took the Beast at his word and made herself at home in the library.

Belle considered books priceless treasures. So when she took a break from reading, she gave the books special attention. She dusted them. She placed fallen books back on the shelves. And she pressed flat any folded pages.

One morning, Belle noticed the Beast had left his favorite book lying open on the arm of his chair. "That's not good for the binding," Belle said.

She picked up the book and examined it. Although the lettered cover was worn, it was a beautiful volume with a brass clasp decorated with pearls. But Belle noticed one of the pearls was missing.

Belle looked around on the floor, in case it had fallen out just then. Chip helped her search. "I found something!" he called.

By the library door was a single perfect pearl.

"Let's see if it fits," Belle suggested. She dropped the pearl into the hole in the clasp.

"It's perfect!" Chip said.

But the pearl was loose and wouldn't stay put.

"I have an idea," Belle said. "This book is obviously the Beast's favorite. I'll fix it up a bit at a time. As the finishing touch, I'll reattach the pearl."

"Then you can surprise him!" Chip cried.

Belle nodded. She was happy to do something nice for the Beast.

Belle got right to work. She borrowed some rags and polish from Mrs. Potts and gently cleaned the book's leather cover. Then she put the book back on the Beast's chair so he wouldn't miss it.

But when the Beast came into the library, he didn't pick up his book. He seemed to be looking for something.

"Can I help?" Belle asked.

"NO!" he bellowed. Then, more quietly, he added, "I mean, no. Excuse me." Without another word, he left the room.

Belle was surprised but shrugged it off, assuming the Beast's bad mood would pass. At least that time he had apologized for his rude behavior.

That afternoon, Belle did some more work on the book. Carefully, she smoothed out rumpled pages and polished the brass clasp.

"I can see myself!" Chip exclaimed.

Again Belle put the book back in its place on the Beast's chair.

Later that evening, Belle passed the Beast in the hall. She smiled and stopped to greet him. "Good evening—"

"Good night!" he snapped, hurrying by.

Belle stood there, a bit stunned. He hadn't even glanced her way. *Is something the matter?* she wondered.

The next morning, it was time for Belle to add the pearl. But she wasn't sure she was ready to give the book to the Beast. He had been so grouchy the day before. *What will he be like today?* she wondered.

Just then, the Beast burst through the door. "You?" he cried. "You've had the pearl all along? I've been looking everywhere trying to find it!"

"Well, why didn't you say so?" Belle shouted. She tossed the pearl onto the table. "By the way, I've been fixing up your book as a surprise."

The Beast was shocked. He looked at the book. He picked up the pearl. Then he smiled—and began to laugh.

Belle stormed toward the door.

"Belle, wait," the Beast said. His gentle voice made Belle stop and turn. "I've been working on something for you, too."

In the Beast's hand was a lovely rose-shaped pin. "It's been in my family a long time," he explained. "I wanted you to have it. But first, I had something to add."

He placed the pearl on the pin, at the base of the rose. It fit perfectly.

"I removed the pearl from my book yesterday," he said. "But I must have dropped it on my way out and—" He looked down. "I'm sorry I blamed you." Then it was Belle's turn to laugh. "Well, I'm sorry I stole your surprise."

Belle pinned the gold rose with the perfect pearl to her dress. Then she watched as the Beast noticed his book's shining brass clasp, polished cover, and smooth pages.

"Thank you, Belle," he said. "You've made it new."

Belle and the Beast still had much to learn about each other. But their hearts were in the right place.

The Quest for the Purple Pearl

"**W**AAAHHHHH!" A voice wailed though King Triton's underwater castle. Swimming by, Ariel stopped. She knew that voice. It was her sister Adella, and she sounded upset!

Ariel swam closer. Adella was sitting next to their sister Aquata.

"You can't let anyone see you. You have a bad case of the bubbles!" Aquata was saying to Adella. "It's from eating too much sugared seaweed."

Adella's face was covered with pink and green polka dots!

"Daddy warned me not to eat too much seaweed," Adella said. "If he sees me, I'll be in so much trouble." She hiccuped, and pink and green bubbles floated up.

Aquata frowned. "Bubbles are serious. There is a cure, but it's almost impossible to find—pearl lotion made from a purple pearl. They grow inside triple-banded sea oysters."

Adella whimpered. "Don't those oysters. . .eat merfolk?"

Ariel bit her lip. Poor Adella needed her help!

Later, in her treasure grotto, Ariel told her fish friend Flounder that she was going to find a purple pearl.

"But the triple-banded sea oysters live in Blackbeard's Trench! That means you'll have to cross the Barbed Sea Kelp Forest," Flounder warned.

"Don't be such a guppy," Ariel said. She swung her collecting sack over her shoulder. "Are you coming?"

Flounder didn't like being called a guppy. So together, he and Ariel headed off to find the purple pearl.

The ocean path leading to the kelp forest was dark. . .and very quiet. Even though Ariel had told Flounder not to be afraid, she started to get cold fins herself as they swam along. Up ahead was the Barbed Sea Kelp Forest, and it looked like a dangerous place!

Even though Ariel was scared, she knew that she had to help her sister! With a flip of her fins, she entered the kelp forest. Cautiously, she swam among the strands, careful not to touch any thorns.

"Let me go ahead," Flounder said, trying to be brave. "I'm smaller than you."

"Good thinking!" Ariel said.

"This way!" Flounder called. He zipped through another gap. But it was too tight for Ariel. A thorn scratched her arm.

Suddenly, Ariel felt the pull of the riptide behind her. The current was getting stronger.

As Ariel watched, the riptide forced the kelp strands apart. That gave her an idea.

"Watch out, Flounder," she cried. "I'm coming through!"

At just the right moment, Ariel launched herself into the rushing water. The current carried her straight through a gap in the kelp without a scratch. She grabbed the anchor of a wrecked ship to stop herself.

Flounder and Ariel continued swimming until a giant crack split the seabed in front of them. They swam down into it, deeper and deeper. Finally, they reached the very bottom of Blackbeard's Trench. All around them, triple-banded sea oysters were scattered like flowers in a strange underwater garden. Their shells were open. Inside each was a shimmering, glowing pearl.

"They don't look very scary," Flounder said. Ariel had to agree.

"Maybe it's just a myth," Ariel said. "I'll just swim in, and—"

"No!" Flounder grabbed Ariel's tail. "We've got to be sure." He took some driftwood and tossed it into the closest oyster's shell.

SNAP! The oyster chomped it in half!

Ariel sighed. How was she going to get one of the pearls without getting hurt? Maybe there was something in her collecting sack that would help. She emptied it out. Inside she found a dinglehopper, two gizmos, a snarfblatt, and a long feather with a pointy tip. Her seagull friend Scuttle had called it a mimbledoodle.

"That's no help!" Flounder said.

But Ariel picked up the feather. "Don't be so sure," she said.

Ariel tied the feather to the end of a stick. She snuck close to one of the oysters. Then she ran the feather gently along its pink inside. The oyster shuddered then sneezed!

The purple pearl shot out of the oyster's mouth and straight into Ariel's hands!

Together, she and Flounder swam back toward home.

Back at the castle, Ariel burst into Adella's room. "I've got it!" she called.

"Got what?" Adella asked. She turned around. Her face was completely clear!

"You're cured!" Ariel exclaimed. "But how? I overheard you and Aquata talking about how bubbles—"

Aquata laughed. "I was joking! Bubbles go away on their own. You didn't believe me, did you?"

Flounder's jaw dropped. But Ariel quickly smiled. "Oh—me? Believe that story? Of course not!" She hid the glowing collecting bag behind her and quickly swam out.

Later Ariel slid the beautiful pearl out of the collecting sack.

She winked at Flounder. "It would have been a shame to turn it into lotion anyway," she said. "And I know a much better place for it than in a bottle."

Flounder grinned. That meant there was going to be a very special addition to Ariel's treasure grotto!

CINDERELLA'S LIFE had changed overnight! One day, she was cleaning and cooking for her stepmother and stepsisters. The next day, she was married to the Prince and living in a palace.

Cinderella loved living there, but sometimes it felt strange to have the royal staff waiting on her. She often wanted to help. In the morning, she would make her own bed before the maids came in.

In the afternoon, she would sometimes invite her maids to join her for tea. Most of all, Cinderella wanted to get to know the royal staff better. She remembered how lonely she'd been at her stepmother's house. She hoped the maids knew that she was their friend. But whenever Cinderella tried to chat with them, they would politely smile and hurry away to finish other chores.

One morning, at breakfast, Cinderella told the Prince that she was worried. "I want to make sure that the servants are happy working here," she said. "But I can't seem to get any of them to talk to me."

"Wouldn't they tell us if something was wrong?" the Prince asked.

Cinderella nodded. "I suppose so. I just wish there was a way to know for certain."

Later that morning, Cinderella had an idea.

First she went to the costume closet and found a wig. Then she headed straight to the maids' quarters. Luckily, no one was there. A few minutes later, Cinderella came out dressed as a member of the royal staff!

A moment later, Cinderella came upon a maid carrying a tub of water.

"Are you new to the castle?" the maid asked Cinderella.

"Actually, I am," Cinderella said as she helped the maid carry the tub to the ballroom. "Do you like working here?"

"Yes, but there are some things I would change," the maid said.

"Like what?" Cinderella asked.

"Like this tub. If only it were on wheels!" the maid said.

Next, Cinderella went to the palace's sewing room.

"These dresses are beautiful," she told the seamstresses as they sewed.

"Gowns are my favorite thing to sew," one seamstress replied. "I just wish we could go to a ball."

"What I wish," said another seamstress, "is that we had more light in here. I can barely see the lace I'm stitching!"

Cinderella's next stop was the banquet hall. Some of the royal staff members were at a long table. They chatted happily as they polished the silver.

"Come join us!" one of the maids called.

Cinderella walked over and examined the gleaming silver.
"This looks like it's been polished already," she said.
"It was, just yesterday," the maid said. "We're supposed to polish it every day."

Soon it was time for lunch. Cinderella followed the maids to the kitchen. She was delighted to see steaming bowls of soup and loaves of crusty bread laid out on a long table.

But just as everyone sat down, a bell rang. The signal meant that one of the royal staff members was needed for a task. A butler got up. He hadn't even had the chance to taste his soup!

How silly! Cinderella thought. *I'm sure it would be easy to plan chores around staff meals. Prudence must have known she was interrupting lunch when she rang the bell.*

Cinderella slipped away from the kitchen to think. She thought of the first maid, with her tub of water. She thought about the low light in the seamstress's quarters and the silver that was polished every day.

The servants were happy working in the palace, but Cinderella knew that, with a few changes, they could be even happier. She had some work to do!

Quickly, Cinderella went to change back into her own clothes. But before she could, she bumped into the Prince. He almost didn't recognize her!

Cinderella told him the whole story. She needed to talk to him, the King, and the Grand Duke.

Cinderella changed, and then they all met in the throne room.

"I had quite an adventure today," Cinderella told them. "I worked alongside the royal staff. And I got some ideas for small changes that would make a big difference."

"What did you have in mind?" the King asked, curious.